W

GREEN TIGER PRESS
Simon & Schuster Building
Rockefeller Center
1230 Avenue of the Americas
New York, New York 10020
Text copyright © 1991 by Tanis Jordan
Illustrations © 1991 by Martin Jordan
First U.S. edition 1992.
All rights reserved including the right of reproduction
in whole or in part in any form.
Originally published in 1991 in Great Britain by Kingfisher Books Ltd.
GREEN TIGER PRESS is an imprint of Simon & Schuster
Manufactured in Hong Kong.
10 9 8 7 6 5 4 3 2 1

Library of Congress Cataloging-in-Publication Data

Jordan, Tanis, 1948–
    Journey of the Red-Eyed Tree Frog / by Tanis Jordan : illustrated
by Martin Jordan.
        p.   cm.
    Summary: A tree frog whose home is threatened by the destruction
of the rain forest makes a long journey to the heart of the Amazon
jungle, encountering many animals along the way, and consults the
Oracle Toad for advice.
    [1. Tree frogs—Fiction. 2. Frogs—Fiction. 3. Rain forests—
Fiction. 4. Rain forest animals—Fiction. 5. Amazon River Valley—
Fiction.] I. Jordan, Martin, 1944– III. II. Title.
P27.J7685Jo   1992
    [E]—dc20   91–29526
    ISBN: 0–671–76903–0   CIP

MARTIN AND TANIS JORDAN

Journey Of the Red-Eyed Tree Frog

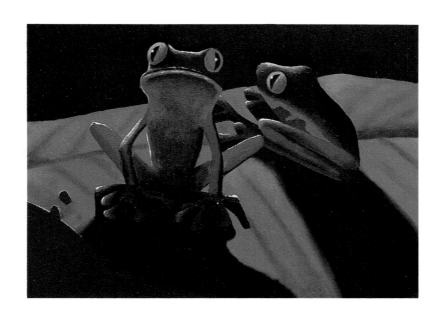

GREEN TIGER PRESS
Published by Simon & Schuster
New York · London · Toronto · Sydney · Tokyo · Singapore

Deep in a Central American forest, on an island in the middle of a wide rushing river, lived two tiny Red-Eyed Treefrogs, Jumps-a-Little and Hops-a-Bit. They made their home in a great Purpleheart tree.

Jumps-a-Little and Hops-a-Bit did not know where the rushing river was going, or why it was in such a hurry to get there. They did not know much at all about the world beyond their island home.

One day, just as sunrise was turning the edges of the Purpleheart leaves to gold, two Toucans stopped by.

"We have come to warn the creatures on this island," they said. "There is danger, great danger. People are coming. They are burning down the forest."

"We have heard of people," said the Treefrogs, "but we have never seen them."

"You will," said the other Toucan. "Already the smoke of their fires is turning the sky black. Climb up, climb up to the top of your Purpleheart tree. Look across the river and you will see."

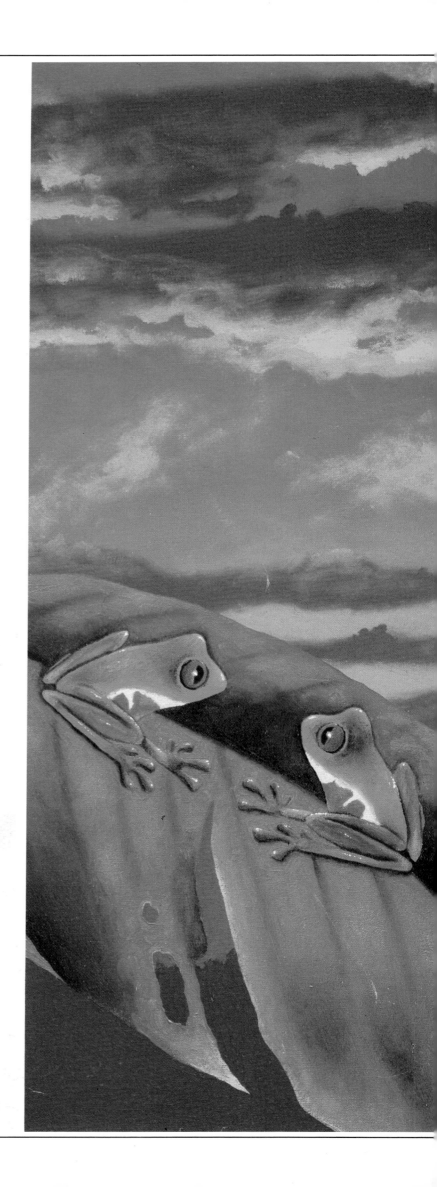

From the topmost leaf of the Purpleheart tree, Jumps-a-Little and Hops-a-Bit saw flames leaping as high as the sky.

A burning wind blew over their moist frog skin and dried it tight across their backs. Sharp smoke stung their eyes.

The two frogs hurried back down the tree.

"Why are the people doing this to our forest?" they asked the Toucans.

"They are building a cattle ranch across the river," answered the Toucans. "They are burning away the trees and bushes to make pastureland."

"Someone must stop them before it's too late," cried Jumps-a-Little.

"It's already too late for us," said the Toucans sadly. "Three days ago, the fire burned up our nest. The people are everywhere. We do not know if they can be stopped."

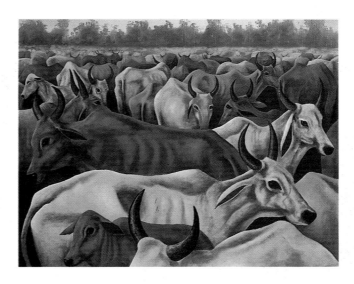

The Toucans and the Treefrogs stared helplessly at each other.

Then, with a sigh, the Toucans stretched out their wings and rose heavily into the burning air. "Goodbye, little Treefrogs," they called. "Good Luck!"

Jumps-a-Little and Hops-a-Bit huddled together. Suddenly a dark shadow fell over them. It was the Atlantic Golden Plover, stopping to rest on her long flight to Canada.

She, too, had seen the forest fires, and the cattle ranches, and the roads, and even the cities the people were building.

"There is only one creature I have met in all my travels who might know what to do," she said. "Deep in the Amazon Rain Forest, far, far from here, lives the Great Wise Toad. He has seen more than any creature I know. Perhaps he can help."

"I must go to him at once!" cried Hops-a-Bit.

"It is a long journey," said Plover, "full of many wonders and many dangers. I do not know if a little frog, even a very brave little frog, can do it."

Then, with a loud flapping of wings, she was gone.

The two Treefrogs dragged a strong leaf to the river and Hops-a-Bit climbed aboard.

"Goodbye!" he called as the leaf swirled into the channel.

The leaf rushed along on the river current. By day, Hops-a-Bit saw wonderful sights – animals and plants he had never known existed. By night, he watched the starry sky glide past.

The river, once clear and green, became thick and oily, smelly and brown. Then Hops-a-Bit saw people. Boats full of them chugged by, filling the air with noise and smoke.

The river flowed on. Hops-a-Bit saw cities and factories. "Oh my," he exclaimed, "the Toucans were right. The people are everywhere! What can stop them now?"

The leaf swirled around a bend in the river, and there was the great, tossing ocean.

"Oh my," cried Hops-a-Bit, "the sea is too big for me and my leaf boat!" He paddled the leaf to shore.

Hops-a-Bit hopped up on a big green rock. Far out to sea, blue water and blue sky melted together. Tumbling waves crashed against the shore.

Suddenly the rock shook. Hops-a-Bit held on with his sticky Treefrog toes. Under his nose, a great golden eye blinked open.

"Why are you sitting on my head?" asked the enormous Green Turtle.

"I thought you were a rock," answered Hops-a-Bit. "I hopped up on you to see what I could see." He told the turtle about the terrible fires in the forest and his journey.

"I was going to ask the Great Wise Toad how to stop them," said Hops-a-Bit. "But this ocean is too rough for my little leaf boat."

"The ocean is not too rough for me," said the turtle. "Hop on my back and I will swim you down the coast."

The turtle lumbered into the surf and dove deep under the waves. Just when Hops-a-Bit thought his lungs would burst, the turtle shot to the surface, swimming south along the coastline.

Out to sea, the ocean billowed and heaved. Seagulls wheeled in the sky, then darted down to splash into the water. "Skree, skree, skree," they called to one another.

On some days the brilliant sun glinted off the tossing waters, making Hops-a-Bit squint. On others, a chilly fog rolled across the sea, blotting out the sun and the land.

At times Hops-a-Bit was sure he could not hold on any longer. But he thought of his island home and of Jumps-a-Little. He remembered the fires in the forest. He tightened his grip on the turtle's shell.

Finally the turtle glided in to the beach. A tear slid from her eye. "Why are you crying," asked Hops-a-Bit. "These are special tears to wash out the extra salt I soak up from the sea," she said. "Now, little frog, the way for you lies overland. Good luck."

Hops-a-Bit hopped along the beach. After a while he found a place just right for a nap.

Chink, chink, chink. A tapping noise woke him up. "Come out of that bottle, little frog," called a huge Jabiru Stork, "before the tide sweeps you out to sea." He told Hops-a-Bit that bottles are dangerous, for they break, leaving pieces of glass that cut and even kill wild creatures.

"This is another way people are hurting our world," said Hops-a-Bit. "I must hurry to the Great Wise Toad."

The Jabiru pointed his long bill toward the mountains beyond the beach. "Over the Andes, little frog," he said. "Over the Andes. Good luck."

High into the Andes Mountains climbed the little Treefrog. The way led across open fields of gray and brown rocks and boulders, stretching up as far as he could see, their edges knife-sharp against the clear blue mountain air.

Now the mountainsides were white – dazzling white snow and ice, shimmering in the cold mountain sunshine. Hops-a-Bit had never seen such whiteness. He had never felt such coldness. He hopped quickly, for his moist frog skin was beginning to freeze.

In the distance, Hops-a-Bit saw smoke rising from a big, square pile of rocks. He hurried along a dirt pathway between the snowfields and found an opening in the rocks. It was warm inside. A small fire burned in a ring of stones. Three furry shapes nestled together in the shadows.

"Who are you, and what is this place?" asked Hops-a-Bit.

"We are guinea pigs," said one of the three. "We belong to the Quechua people, and we live here, in their warm hut."

Hops-a-Bit told the guinea pigs about his journey.

"Stay here for the night," said the black and white guinea pig. "We will keep you warm until the sun returns."

The guinea pigs gathered around Hops-a-Bit, making a warm, furry nest with their bodies. Snuggled among them, he quickly fell asleep.

Early in the morning, Hops-a-Bit said goodbye to the guinea pigs. Down through ice and snow fields, down through rock and boulder fields, down through grassy scrubland he hopped. Far below, he saw clouds floating among the treetops. "Oh my," said Hops-a-Bit, "I have been higher than the sky!"

Down he went, into the misty Cloud Forest. The ground was covered with wet, squashy moss. Vines and creepers grew from tree to tree, making tangled pathways in the air.

Hops-a-Bit climbed up on a vine and stared into the shadowy forest with his red Treefrog eyes. Which way should he go? Suddenly, he heard a rustling in the underbrush. The leafy branches in front of him began to wave and shake. A large, furry animal rose up out of the bushes. Hops-a-Bit jumped with fright.

"Don't be afraid, little frog," she said. "I'm a Spectacled Bear. I won't hurt you."

Hops-a-Bit told the friendly bear about his journey. "Do you know the way to the Great Wise Toad?" he asked.

"Down the mountain, down the mountain," answered the bear. "Good luck!" Then she climbed up to her nest at the top of the tree.

Night came. The moon shone faintly through the clouds and the treetops. The forest was alive with strange sounds. Hops-a-Bit thought longingly of Jumps-a-Little and the Purpleheart tree in his faraway island home.

"Whooo, whooo?" called a voice.

"Hops-a-Bit," he answered nervously, staring into the darkness.

"Whooo, whooo?" called another, screechy voice, even closer to the Treefrog.

There was a loud flapping of wings. Branches rustled and shook as night birds landed all around him.

"Whooo?" said one of the birds again, a Great Horned Owl with wide staring yellow eyes.

When they heard the story of Hops-a-Bit's journey, the owls blinked their large shining eyes at one another. "Follow the stream," they said. "But hurry; go now. Follow the stream until it becomes a river."

"But how will I find the stream?" asked Hops-a-Bit.

"I will take you," said a voice. A dark furry creature landed on the branch next to Hops-a-Bit. "I am a Douracouli Monkey. I can see at night like the owls. Follow me."

The monkey began to swing quickly along the vines. "Keep up, keep up, little frog" he called over his shoulder, "or you'll be lost in the forest!"

The little Treefrog hurried through the dark tangled forest after the monkey. But the monkey's arms were long, and his big bright eyes quick to see the way through the forest blackness.

"Wait, wait!" cried Hops-a-Bit. "I can't keep up!"

But the monkey was already too far ahead. He disappeared into the darkness. There was nothing for Hops-a-Bit to do but hop on alone.

All night long, rustlings and scrapings, shrieks and chatters filled the night air.

Shadowy shapes moved across the forest floor beneath him and swung through the vines and branches about him.

Once in a while, he caught a glimpse of the moon through the branches. Slowly it floated across the sky, and finally sank behind the mountain peaks. The first rays of the sun lit up the treetops.

All at once Hops-a-Bit was surrounded by a flock of birds. A yellow-eyed Harpy Eagle clicked his sharp curved beak at him. A beady-eyed Vulture shook his floppy wattle at him. A Tufted Coquette, no bigger than Hops-a-Bit, poked at him with her needle-sharp beak. A Scarlet Macaw and a Hyacinth Macaw laughed, "Caw, Caw, Caw!"

"Stop, stop," cried Hops-a-Bit. "I am on an important journey." And he told them of his mission.

"We do not like intruders in our forest," said the Harpy Eagle, "not even little frogs. But we don't want people here either, so we will help you on your journey."

With that, the Harpy Eagle picked up Hops-a-Bit in his talons and flew off.

The Harpy Eagle placed him gently on the ground where the stream joined the Amazon River. "Follow the water's flow," said the Eagle, spreading his great wings and rising up on the wind.

"Follow the water's flow. Good luck, little frog."

Hops-a-Bit sat quietly by the bank of the wide river, gathering his thoughts. All around him, the riverbank was waking to the new day.

A scaly gray armadillo went shuffling past his perch.

Then came frogs, hundreds of them, everywhere he looked – red ones and yellow ones, spotted ones and striped ones, big ones and little ones. They chirruped and croaked, warbled and whistled, gargled and glugged.

"Oh my," said Hops-a-Bit, "I didn't know there were so many kinds of frogs in the world. Jumps-a-Little will never believe me!"

He thought of his home in the Purpleheart tree. "Beep," he said sadly to himself and he set off along the river's edge, following the water's flow.

Suddenly a big hairy hand reached down from a tree and scooped him up.

Staring at him was the strangest creature he had yet seen on his long journey, a very hairy monkey with a hairless head and a face almost as red as Hops-a-Bit's own red Treefrog eyes.

"Who are you?" said Hops-a-Bit.

"He's a Red-faced Uakari. You say it like wackery," roared a loud voice in his ear.

"What are you doing here, Howler Monkey?" screamed the Red-faced Uakari, his face getting redder and redder. "This is my territory."

"It's mine, it's mine," roared the Howler Monkey. "Get away, you Red-faced Uakari!"

"Get away, you Howler Monkey!"

"Get away, you Red-faced Uakari!"

The monkeys were so busy shrieking at each other that neither of them noticed Hops-a-Bit quietly crawl down the tree trunk and hop away into the underbrush.

"Oh my," panted Hops-a-Bit, hurrying along the riverbank as fast as he could hop, "there are too many surprises on this journey. Where, oh where, is the Great Wise Toad?"

He climbed up a Cecropia tree to see what he could see. What he saw was a gray Sloth, hanging from a vine, baby snuggled against her, smiling gently at all the world about her.

Hops-a-Bit hung upside down to ask about the Great Wise Toad.

"You are nearly there, little frog," answered the sloth. "The Great Wise Toad lives just across the river."

"Haw, haw, haw," laughed a blue and yellow Macaw, also hanging upside down. "How can a little frog cross such a wide river?"

But Hops-a-Bit had already picked a large leaf and climbed onto it. "This part will be easy," he said. "I've done it before."

And he launched himself out onto the river.

Hops-a-Bit paddled hard with his front feet. But the strong current began to pull the leaf down the river.

"Oh my," cried Hops-a-Bit, "I'll be swept right past the home of the Great Wise Toad!"

Four Piranhas, sharp triangular teeth gleaming, swam in circles around his leaf. An Electric Eel and a Stingray lurked just below. Suddenly, a giant Catfish came looming out of the depths, nearly upsetting the leaf.

Then three shining Tetra fish came to the rescue. Pushing their noses against the leaf and lashing their tails, they swam for

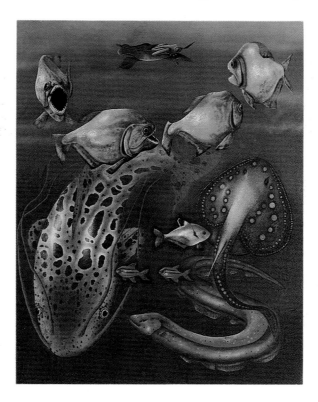

the bank with all their might. They gave the leaf one last push, dove under the water, and were gone.

The leaf glided through an opening in the bank and floated into a dark, still, secret lagoon. Hops-a-Bit looked across the lagoon and drew his breath.

Three powerful jungle cats, as still and mysterious as the lagoon itself, watched him from the shadows.

"So, little frog," purred the Jaguar, "at last you are here. We have been waiting for you."

"How did you know I was coming?" asked a very surprised Hops-a-Bit.

"All the Rain Forest speaks of your journey," answered the Black Jaguar.

"I seek the Great Wise Toad," said Hops-a-Bit.

"You shall find him, little frog," said the golden Jaguar. Tomorrow, at sunrise, the Ocelot will take you to him. Tonight, you will stay in the lagoon where you will be safe."

The Jaguars told Hops-a-Bit that people were a threat to them as well. Poachers were hunting them to turn their beautiful skins into fur coats for people to wear.

Tears came to Hops-a-Bit's eyes. Now that he was nearly at the end of his long journey, he felt very small and afraid. The bright hope that had carried him along the rushing river, down the stormy coastline, high over the Andes Mountains and through the dark tangly forests suddenly dimmed.

The great cats seemed to know how he felt. "You are small, little frog," said the Black Jaguar, "but you have shown you have a great heart. Do not give up now."

Just before dawn, Hops-a-Bit climbed on the back of the Ocelot. Silently they slipped through the underbrush along the dark riverbank to the foot of a great rock. "Wait here," said the Ocelot, and she disappeared into the shadows.

The dark sky glowed, pale peach, as the sun began to rise. Hops-a-Bit shivered. As the sun's rays struck the water, the mist cleared, and there, on the top of the rock, sat the Great Wise Toad.

"Come here to me, little Hops-a-Bit," he called.

Trembling, Hops-a-Bit climbed slowly up the rock. The Great Wise Toad was the most striking creature he had ever seen. His warty skin glowed amber in the dawn light. His golden eyes shone.

"O Great Wise Toad," began Hops-a-Bit – and then he fell silent. What could he say to this awesome creature who knew everything that ever could be known?

"I know, little frog," said the Great Wise Toad. "You have come about the problem of the people. The world belongs to all creatures, including the people. But too many people want it all for themselves. We do not have the power to stop them."

"Then is there nothing to be done?" gasped Hops-a-Bit, finding his voice. "Has my journey been for nothing?"

"Oh, no, little frog, not for nothing, not for nothing," said the Great Wise Toad. "There are already people who know that the world is to be shared. What you have done will make more people want to share, especially the children. They can make a better future for all the world's creatures. When they hear your story, the children will understand and take better care of our world."

"But what about now?" cried Hops-a-Bit. "What about the fires? What about my island? What about Jumps-a-Little?"

"Your home is safe," said the Great Wise Toad. "Caring people have found your beautiful island and made it a protected place."

"My island is safe," said Hops-a-Bit, leaping with happiness. "But, oh my, how shall I get home. I do not think I can hop any more."

The Great Wise Toad laughed. "You will not have to hop any more," she said. "Here is your old friend the Atlantic Golden Plover to carry you home."

The Atlantic Golden Plover swooped down from a Brazilnut Tree. She curled her long gray toes gently around Hops-a-Bit.

"Little Treefrog," said the Great Wise Toad, "you have hopped much to help your friends. No longer will you be called Hops-a-Bit. I give you the name of Hops-a-Lot."

"Hops-a-Lot," whispered the little Treefrog to himself. "Hops-a-Lot." It seemed to fit. "Thank you, Great Wise Toad," called Hops-a-Lot, as the Golden Plover stretched her wings and carried him into the air. "Goodbye, goodbye."

Once he was home, Hops-a-Lot and Jumps-a-Little sat together in their favorite Purpleheart tree watching the sun set beyond the wide rushing river.

A band of White-Lipped Peccaries grazed nearby. A Tapir and her baby wandered by on their way home.

"Beep," went Hops-a-Lot. "Beep," went Jumps-a-Little.

Hops-a-Lot remembered the long, lonely nights of his journey. How glad he was to be here with Jumps-a-Little, safe in the branches of the Purpleheart tree.

He sighed happily. Although he had seen many amazing creatures and his journey had been full of adventure, nothing could ever be so wonderful as his own little island home.